This
Harry and
the
Dinosaurs
book belongs to

. . . .

For Edward Matthew Traynor
I.W.

For Aonghas and Mairead
A.R.

PUFFIN BOOKS

UK | USA | Canada | Ireland | Australia
India | New Zealand | South Africa

Puffin Books is part of the Penguin Random House group of companies
whose addresses can be found at global.penguinrandomhouse.com.

www.penguin.co.uk   www.puffin.co.uk   www.ladybird.co.uk

First published 2004
This edition published 2016
001

Text copyright © Ian Whybrow, 2004
Illustrations copyright © Adrian Reynolds, 2004
All rights reserved
The moral right of the author and illustrator has been asserted

Made and printed in China

ISBN: 978-0-141-37509-0

All correspondence to:
Puffin Books
Penguin Random House Children's
80 Strand, London WC2R 0RL

Harry and the Dinosaurs at the Museum

Ian Whybrow **Adrian Reynolds**

PUFFIN

Sam wanted Mum to take her to the museum.
She had to study the Romans for homework.
"What are Romans?" asked Harry.

Sam said they were our ancestors, but he was
too young to understand.
  Harry wanted to take the dinosaurs to see them.

Sam said, "No way!"
She said Harry would just get bored and silly.
That was why Sam's homework got smudged.

Mum made them both settle down.
She said a museum would be a fine
outing for everybody.
  "I'd love to go," said Nan.

The museum was bigger than a hospital.
You had to have a map.

On the way to the Romans, they passed the cavemen.
  "Are these ancestors?" asked Harry.
  Mum said yes, everybody in the world came from cavemen.
They lit fires and did hunting.
  Harry liked the stone axes!

The dinosaurs liked the
sabre-toothed tiger!
Raaah! Sharp teeth!

Next stop was the Egyptians.

They saw mummies in boxes and funny writing like pictures.

"Are Egyptians ancestors?" asked Harry.

"Yes, but not the right ones," said Sam. "We want the Romans. Come on, hurry up!"

Finally they reached the Romans.
They had good swords and spears,
and helmets with brushes on.

But what a lot of old pots, broken ones too!
   Sam started doing drawing.
   "We've seen the Romans now," said Harry.
"I'm hungry! Let's go!"

"Raaah! Anchisaurus pinched me!" said Stegosaurus.
"He's taking up all the room!" said Anchisaurus.
"Behave!" said Harry in a loud voice.
"Look, Harry *is* being silly!" groaned Sam. "I knew it!"

"I think the dinosaurs need a run about," said Harry.
Mum said better not. They might get lost.
"Come on, let's get something to eat," she said.
"Afterwards we'll come back here, so Sam
can finish her studies."

The cafeteria was very busy. Nan and Harry
and the dinosaurs waited at a table while
Mum and Sam went to queue up.

"Look, I'm a caveman! Raaah!" said Triceratops.
"Look, I'm a Roman! Raaah!" said Pterodactyl.
"Look, I'm a mummy! Raaah!" said Tyrannosaurus.

After lunch, everyone felt a lot better and they set off back to the Romans.

But it wasn't long before Anchisaurus got bored. "I'm bored too!" said Tyrannosaurus.

"Never mind," said Harry, "it's your turn to do studying. Pay attention, my dinosaurs."

He taught them Climbing Up Display Cases. Then taught them Sliding On The Slippery Floor.

That was how they got lost.

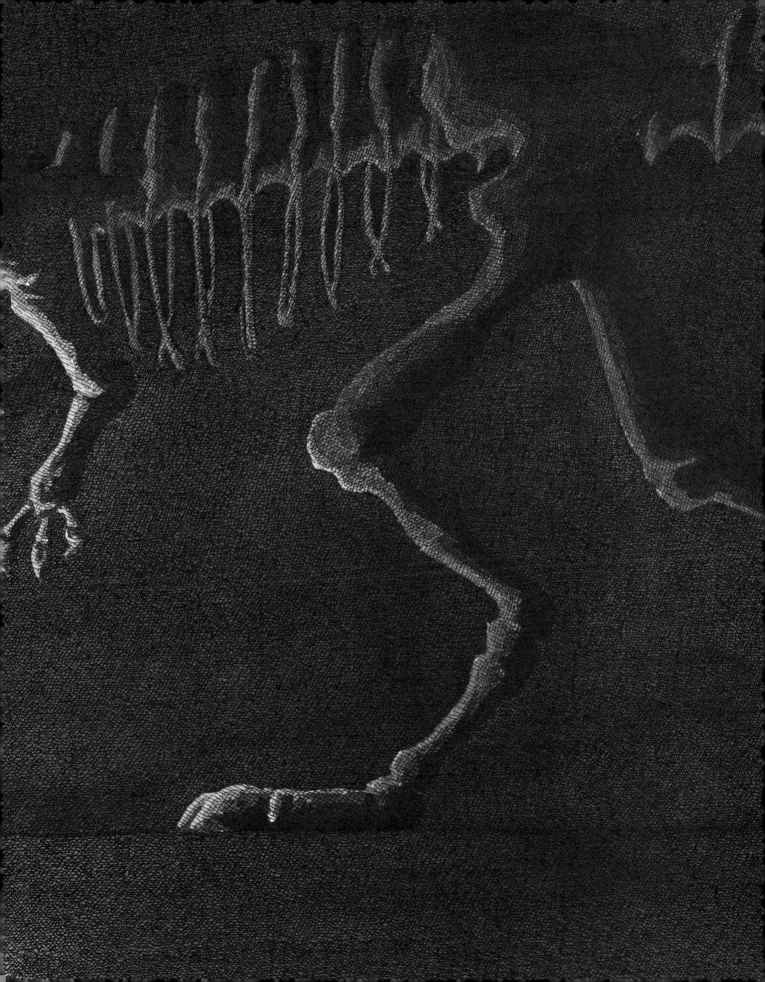

"Oh no! Where's Harry?" said Mum. "Quick!
Let's find the person in charge!"

Sam said Harry was stupid. "I bet he's gone off
on a bus!" she said.

"Nonsense!" said Nan. "I know where
we'll find him!"

They followed Nan to the Prehistoric Hall.
"There he is!" said Nan. "I knew it!"

Harry was still teaching his dinosaurs.
"Boys come from cavemen and Romans and Egyptians,"
he explained. "But these are *your* ancestors."

So Tyrannosaurus said "Raaah!" to his ancestor.
So did Apatosaurus and Scelidosaurus and Triceratops
and the rest of the bucketful of dinosaurs.
All except Pterodactyl, who gave his ancestor a nose-rub.

"Now, young man!" said the person in charge. "We had better look for your mum. Could you tell me your name?"

Harry said his name, address and telephone number, no problem at all.
All the people said very good, clever boy!
Nan rushed over. "He's with us!" she called proudly.

"Harry!" said Mum. "We thought we'd lost you!"

"I wasn't lost!" said Harry. "I was with my dinosaurs."

"And we were with our ancestors," said the dinosaurs. RAAAAH!

ENDOSAURUS

SCELIDOSAURUS

(ske-LI-doh-SAW-rus)

TYRANNOSAURUS

(tie-RAN-oh-SAW-rus)

TRICERATOPS

(try-SER-a-tops)

STEGOSAURUS

(STEG-oh-SAW-rus)

PTERODACTYL

(TER-oh-DAC-til)

APATOSAURUS

(a-PAT-oh-SAW-rus)

ANCHISAURUS

(AN-ki-SAW-rus)